The Burger and the Hot Dog

To the California Raisins, with love
—J. A.

Atheneum Books for Young Readers
An imprint of Simon & Schuster Children's Publishing Division
1230 Avenue of the Americas
New York, New York 10020

Book design by Ann Bobco
The text of this book was set in Adobe Garamond.
The illustrations were rendered in colored pencil, watercolor, pastel, crayon, and coffee.

Printed in Hong Kong

10 9 8 7 6 5 4 3 2 1

Library of Congress Cataloging-in-Publication Data
Aylesworth, Jim.
The burger and the hot dog / written by Jim Aylesworth ; illustrated by Stephen Gammell.—1st ed.
p.   cm.
ISBN 0-689-83897-2
1. Food—Juvenile poetry. 2. Children's poetry, American. [1. Food—Poetry.
2. American poetry.] I. Gammell, Stephen, ill. II. Title.
PS3551.Y58 F66 2001
811'.54—dc21   00-040152

FIRST
EDITION

this book is called THE BURGER and the HOT DOG

written by JIM AYLESWORTH

pictures by STEPHEN GAMMELL

(two good apples)

atheneum books for young readers

NEW YORK   LONDON   TORONTO   SYDNEY   SINGAPORE

So Pretty!

"You're pretty!" said an orange
To a lemon, who seemed pleased.
"In fact, my dear, so pretty,
You're at risk of getting squeezed!"

Veggie Soup

Carl Carrot is lead singer
In a band called Veggie Soup.
They're old-time country/western,
And they're quite a well-known group.

Bo Beet, he plays the fiddle.
He's the best, folks say, by far.
Oz Onion, he's on banjo,
And Tex Tater plays guitar.

They all wear fringe and rhinestones,
Fancy hats and cowboy boots,
And everybody loves 'em,
From young kids to real old coots.

Bums

A bunch of sugar cookies
Met a bagel on the street.
Then how they started acting
Proved some cookies aren't so sweet.

These cookies started teasing,
Calling names and making fun.
And then they started chasing
As the guy began to run.

Then something awful happened!
But it served them right, those bums!
They tripped while they were chasing,
And so now they're cookie crumbs!

How Bleak

A stick of gum was standing
'Neath a diner stool last week.
He happened to look upward,
And he said, "Oh, gosh! How bleak!

"I used to know those fellas.
They were sticks once, same as me.
But now they're wads just stuck there,
And it's not so nice to see!"

Yack and Yimmy

Two eggs named Yack and Yimmy
Are both very yolly guys.
With them there's lots of laughing,
And most often some surprise.

They're great to have at parties,
And they're asked by lots of folks.
They keep a party yumping
'Cause they're both so full of yolks.

Too Shy

A hard-boiled egg named Betty,
Who is very, very shy,
Got asked to do some dancing
By a friendly French toast guy.

But Betty said, "No, thank you."
Though just why is hard to tell.
It seems she'll do no dancin'
Till she comes out of her shell.

Don't Worry

An upset boy banana
Said, "Those jerks are hard to bear!
I wave and call, 'Good morning,'
But they act like I'm not there!"

His sister said, "Don't worry.
It's not you, so just relax.
You'd see if you'd look closer
That that bunch is made of wax."

The Burger and the Hot Dog

A burger and a hot dog
One day had a nasty spat.
The burger got insulted
'Cause the hot dog called him flat.

The burger started crying;
His young feelings were all hurt.
So he ran and shoved the hot dog,
Who fell facedown in the dirt.

The hot dog, too, got angry,
And he started talking tough.
Soon both of them were yelling,
And they started throwing stuff.

The soda, who was watching,
Said, "You're both the guilty ones,
And if you do not stop it,
I will kick you in the buns!"

Bacon Buddies

A strip of crispy bacon
Met a buddy not yet cooked.
The raw one said, "My goodness!
You were taller last I looked!"

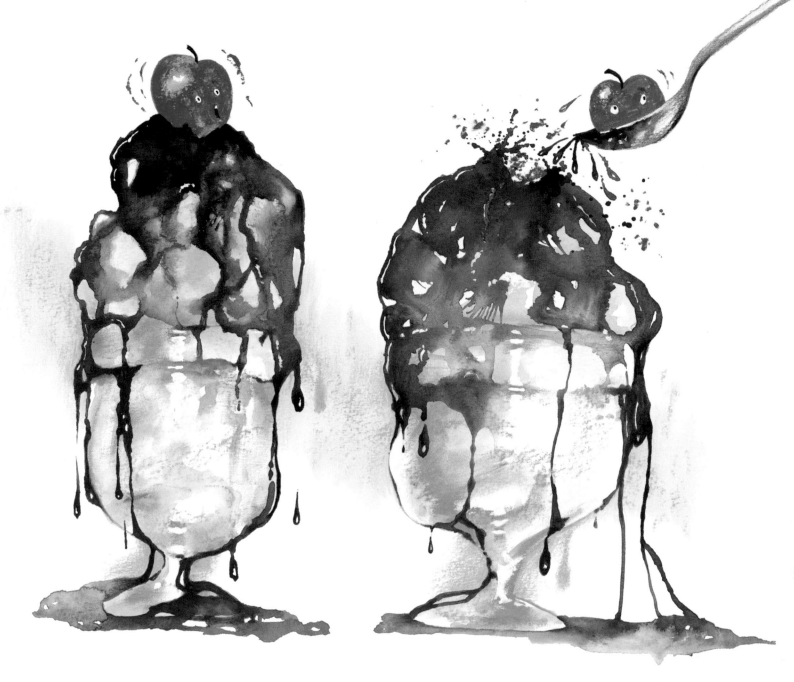

TOP SPOT

When people serve a sundae,
There's a cherry on the top.
But if you ask the cherries,
They'll all wish that that would stop.

They'll say, "Top spot's no honor!
Of all spots, top spot's the worst!"
They've learned from observation
That that top spot's eaten first!

Poor Bar

An ice-cream bar got stranded
On the beach, out in the sun.
The temperature was ninety,
Someone shouted, "Better run!"

But, sadly, though he didn't.
This poor bar was not so quick,
And when his friends next saw him,
He was nothing but a stick.

Bopping Corn

Two ears of corn from Fargo
Love that old-time rock and roll.
They love those sixties dances,
Like the Pony and the Stroll.

Last night they played some records;
Did the Twist, and then they bopped.
But got so overheated,
That before they knew, they popped.

Overpriced

One night Bert Beef Bologna
Switched the numbers on his tag.
The change made him expensive,
But his purpose was no gag.

Bert hoped to fool the shoppers,
Who would think him overpriced.
And then they wouldn't buy him,
And he'd put off getting sliced.

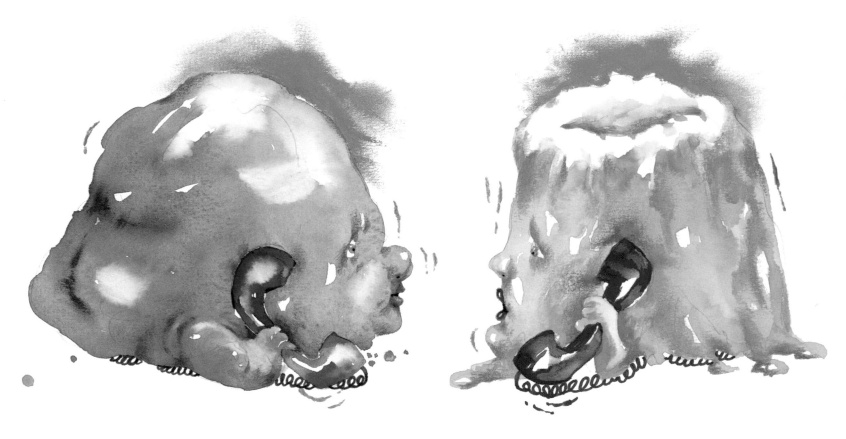

Angel Cake

An angel cake in Kansas
Once phoned up her boyfriend bread.
"Come take me out to dinner,"
Is, in short, just what she said.

The bread said, "You're my sweetie,
And you know I love you so,
But restaurants are expensive!
You must think I'm made of dough!"

Blueberries

Stu bumped into two berries.
One was Bruce, the other Brad.
They both sat there together.
Both were looking rather sad.

Stu asked them, "What's the matter?"
Is there something I can do?"
Bruce answered rather glumly,
"We are both just feeling blue."

sticky Buns

Cinnamon buns in Cincy
Are those very gooey types
Which causes them big troubles,
That result in bun-type gripes.

"We're sick of being sticky!"
Griped one bun as he walked by.
"You said it!" said another.
Still another griped, "No lie!"

"We can't shake hands!" "No, never!"
"Simple hugs just can't be done!"
"And should we bump together,
Oh, my, no, that's never fun!"

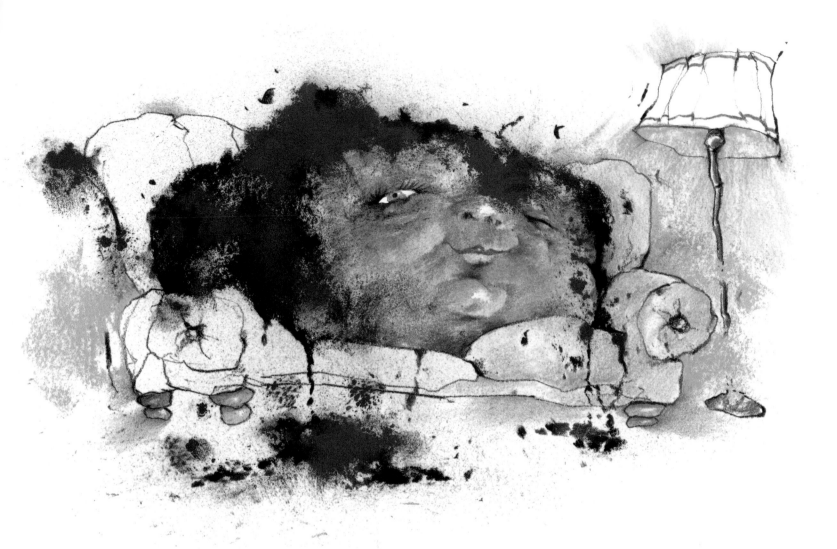

Barb Brownie

Barb Brownie's always sittin',
From her couch, she doesn't budge.
It's not that she is nutty,
But just weighted down with fudge.

Nellie and Bill

Two pickles went out dancing:
She a gherkin, he a dill.
The gherkin's name was Nelly,
And her partner, he was Bill.

That dill Bill was so sour
That the evening seemed quite long.
Still Nelly kept on smiling,
And she danced to every song.

For sure, she's no complainer;
Even though Bill mashed her feet.
That's why I like her better!
She's more pleasant 'cause she's sweet!

The Perfect Couple

A wedge of cheese named Woodrow
Has a smell which does offend.
In fact, it is so awful
That he hardly has a friend.

And sure, it hurts his feelings
When folks run and yell, "pee-you!"
But who can really blame them?
And I think you'd do it, too.

For years, he was so lonely
That he'd sit at home and cry.
But never could he change it.
He was just a stinky guy.

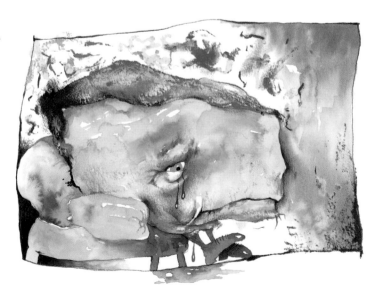

Then last week, he met Wanda,
Quite a pungent wedge as well.
Now they're the perfect couple,
'Cause they neither one can tell.

Floozies

Justine's a just-cheese pizza
With a thin and crispy crust.
She'll never add on toppings,
Saying, "That won't be discussed!"

"I'm just a plain cheese pizza,
Which I argue is the best.
Those other gals are floozies
Who are always overdressed!"

Gripes

Most candy canes are happy,
But today I heard some gripes:
Two lady canes were saying
They were sick of wearing stripes.

Frankie Fish Stick

Don't sell him short, not Frankie.
Though a fish stick, he's no fool.
You'll note by that diploma,
He did well when back in school.

Up To You

These food folks live in my town,
And they also live in yours.
Some families have so many
That they've started giving tours.

I know at least one hundred,
But there are lots I've not yet met;
Like Tess the Taffy Apple,
And a nutmeg named Nanette.

So keep your eyes wide open!
You'll meet new ones if you do,
But if you want more poems,
Then the rhyming's up to you!